All the Colors of the Race

All the Colors of the Race

Poems by Arnold Adoff
Illustrated by John Steptoe

Lothrop, Lee & Shepard Books
New York

All the colors of the race

All the colors of the race
are
      in my face, and just behind my face:
               behind my eyes:
      inside my head.

And inside my head, I give my self a place
      at the end of a long
           line   forming
               it self into a
                  circle.

And I am holding out my hands.

I think the real color   is behind the color

I think the real color   is behind the color.
That
skin on
        my face   is for the cold mornings,
        and
        the cool breezes of some
                        summer afternoons.

Under that skin   and under that
                        face
            is the real
                race.

Past

I have all these parts   stuffed in
                                me
like mama's chicken
                and
            biscuits,
                and
daddy's apple pie, and a tasty
                        story
from the family
            tree.

But I know that tomorrow
                morning
        I'll wake up
            empty, and hungry for that
                                next
                                bite
        of my new
            day.

Great Grandma Ida

Great Grandma Ida came from a small village
in Poland
        on the Russian border.
        And her parents came
                from that same village.
And their parents before them.

And sometime, long before that,
                these
people came from Spain.
        And a long
           time before that,
                those
people had come from places
                in the Middle
                    East
                or Africa,
across the Mediterranean Sea.

Borders

Great Grandma Ida came from a small village
in Poland
>
> on the Russian border
> to America,
> on a ship that   sailed
> for weeks,
> on the rough Atlantic
>> Ocean:

to make a new place for her self;
to work in a factory; to find her father;
to find a man
>
> from a German town on the Polish
>> border

to marry; to have and raise a daughter
> who would find and marry
> a man from a Russian town
>> on the Polish
>> border.

And in 1935 they would have a baby boy
> in a New York City hospital
who is daddy now to
> me.

I know we can go back so far

We can go back so far
so far
but only so far
and
not as far as forward.

One Great Grandma's family   was lost to us,
        when they were marched to the Nazi death
camps
        and their Polish town destroyed.

One Great Grandma's family was lost to us
        in the years of slavery,
        and in the Civil War
        smoke of burning plantations.

I am making a circle for my self

I am making a circle for my self
                              and
I am placing into that
                circle: all who are for me,
                        and
                        all   that is inside.

If I am only   white and Jewish   then mama stays
                                                outside.
If I am only   black and Protestant
                                then daddy stays
                                        outside.

But Golda is in the circle. Ben Gurion. Moses.
And Grandpa Jack is
                surely
                in.

I am making a circle for my self
                              and
I am placing into
            that circle: all who are for me;
                        all that is inside
                                    me.

If I am only black and Protestant:
            then daddy stays outside.
If I am only white and Jewish:
            then mama stays outside.

But Harriet is in the circle. Martin King. Malcolm.
And Great
        Grandpa Perry is
                    surely
                in.

Still finding out

Finding out that Grandpa Perry
was
born a slave   and died a free
farmer
here in Ohio:
I am
free
here in Ohio
on the Perry land: planting tomatoes
on his same land.

I am part Perry
and
part still
finding
out.

I am

Mama is black
          and
          daddy
          is white
and
I am black
and
I am white:

          besides
my age
     and
     sex
     and
          clarinet.

Flavors

Mama is chocolate: you must be swirls
                            of dark fudge,
                    and ripples
                                  through
                    your cocoa
                            curls;
chips
        and
flips of sprinkles
        on your
                summer
                face.

Flavors

Daddy is vanilla: you must be mean
                                    old
                          bean
                in the morning,
                cherry
                chunks by afternoon,
                and
                        sweet
                        peach sometimes.

But mostly   you
                are vanilla
                          up
                your
                arms.

Flavors

Me
is better
   butter: I must be
                    pecans
                           roasted,
                           toasted;
almond
wal nut   three
       scoop combination
                 cone:
melting under
      kisses.

It is a new color.
It is a new flavor.
      For
       love.

On my applications

On my applications   I can
                            put:
this girl:
        a black,
            white,
Christian,
Jewish,
        young
        woman:
            student,
            musician,
singer,
dancer,
runner   in the middle distance races,

        is willing to help you
        if you take her as she
                            is.

Trilingual

I can talk
          black,
  and
I can talk
          white,
  and
I can talk
        so no
        one
understands.

Four
Foot
Feat

Imagine I am standing with
                    one
                        foot
in Africa: for my
                    ancestors
dragged away from their
homes and lands and tribes
to sail to
            America as
                        slaves.

                        One
                            foot
in Europe: for my
                    ancestors
living in their ghettos, in
their Polish and German
villages, until they
                        sailed
to America to find
a new home and
                life.

Imagine I am standing with
                    one
                    foot
in New York City: for my
first eight years of
                    riding
the Central Park carousel;
walking on Broadway;
                    listening
to the music
          of the streets.

                    One
                    foot
in Ohio: for my present
time of summer corn
and the smell of hogs
          after rain.
                    This
                    town
has birds that bring
the mornings to my
          room.

Four foot feat: enough to make me sit
                    right down.

The lady said:

The lady said: what are you going to
                                 be
         when you grow
         all the way up?

And I said: a woman.

And she said.   No. I mean what are
                      you
                    now?
And I said: a girl.

And she said: No. I mean what do you call
                         yourself?
And I said: Honey. Baby. Sweet
              potato
              pie
                    face me.

If she finds it hard,
        I find it easy
   to make it hard for her.

I know the rules

I know the rules   and I am what I am
                                   because
            I can say
                  what I am,
           and what I need,
           and what I hope to become
                            in this world.
That is the rule I add for me.

My eyes can see
           and lips smile
           and lips kiss.

Arms can stretch out
                and
        circle:
              hold
              and
              hug.

There is so much

There is so much
in the way we all live
that
      separates: it must be hard
                         for some people
to see
daddy reaching over
                  me
to kiss
mama in the grocery,
or see
mama laugh
      and hug
            daddy
      in the street.

Bad guys

We live the same: our way,
and walk
　　　　the same;
and talk,
　　　　no matter where we live
　　　　　　　　and go.
And most people
smile at us　　on sunny Ohio afternoons
　　　　in　parks　and　restaurants.
But
while we talk and smile
and eat
　　our way through
　　　　Sundays, we keep a corner
　　　　　　of our eyes　　for
　　　　　　　　　　any

　　　　bad guys.

Some old ones

Some old ones   talk about:
                              this one
                  is
                  so dark,
and
      that
one   is
        so light,   and
                          this
                  one
has such
      hair.

But the young ones
                    talk about:
                              brothers
                                    and
                              sisters.

Passing

        they called it
             in the old days:
supposed to
     be millions
        crossed that magic
              line:
to live as white;
to give up the daily struggle
   for good:
   give up grandmas   and the   land.

Can we wipe it with our lives?
Can we wipe it the way you
      wipe a chalk line
     with your
        hand?
Or is
   it running up my spine?

I was Harriet

I was Harriet
in
   the   play

   and

      got
   to   lead
      them
   all
      to
      free
   dom.

At the meeting

At the meeting
              they said they wanted to send
one white
         and one black kid to the celebration,
to make it even and equal.
So
I said to just send me   and it would still be
                                        fair,
and we could still
         save one round-trip fare.

Then they waited to see if I was smiling
before they laughed,
and my motion lost because I forgot
              I couldn't be a boy.

We are talking about

We are talking about
$\quad\quad\quad\quad$ the ones who pick $\quad$ their friends
$\quad\quad\quad\quad$ because of how $\quad$ black $\quad$ they $\quad$ act
$\quad\quad\quad\quad\quad\quad\quad\quad\quad\quad\quad\quad\quad\quad\quad$ or
$\quad\quad\quad\quad$ because of how $\quad$ white $\quad$ they can
$\quad\quad\quad\quad\quad\quad\quad\quad\quad\quad\quad\quad\quad\quad\quad$ be.

Sometimes blackness seems too black for me,
$\quad\quad\quad$ and whiteness is too $\quad$ sickly pale;
$\quad\quad\quad$ and I wish every
$\quad\quad\quad\quad\quad\quad$ one were golden from
$\quad\quad\quad\quad\quad\quad\quad\quad\quad\quad$ the
$\quad\quad\quad\quad\quad\quad\quad\quad\quad\quad$ sun.
$\quad\quad$ Golden from the
$\quad\quad\quad\quad\quad\quad$ inside
$\quad\quad\quad$ out.

In our one family

In our one family, around
this
round
table
of our nights and days:
we are together
in old ways,
we are together
in new ways.

Pancakes and chicken. Pork chops and cream:
we
are new people
eating our way
to a new time
of
love.
We are trying for the
dream.

When they asked

When they asked
if
I was black or white
            or   what,
I said:
I was black and
                white
            and what
difference
did it make to them.

And they said:
did I have the answers
                to the math
                problems?
And
I had the answers.

Sum People

The   black   man
                 said
I was a   half
                 breed,
but I told
                 him
to
check   out   his
                 math:
like
          one
                    plus
     one.

A song:

I have the fore
head
of the black
Ohio
farmers
looking
at the
sky
for rain.

Baby
Blue.

And my nose
has   that Russian
Jewish
bump.

Jump.

I can do my hair

I can do my hair   short
                           and
                     curled
                       tight
on my head,
or let it
        grow
        long, and wave it
              like the
                        rest
        of my friends.

I look in the mirror
and see
      me standing with a brush.
I have just arrived.
I am in a rush. I want to be
                          the
                          best.

If they hate me

If they hate me
  they
are
  sick
and
  hurt
and
  need
  some
  kind
of
  help.

I will
  stay
right
  here.

For every one

For every one   we know the inside
                                blood
                                is
                                    blue:
and when we cut,
            or scrape,
            or scratch
                        below the skin
the outside blood
                    is red:
                    is red for every
                                one.

True: red for every one.

A song:

I am of the earth   and the earth is of me.
I am all the colors of the corn field,
                    and the corn field
   is all the colors of me.
I am all the colors of the plowed-up garden,
                    and the plowed-up garden
   is all the colors of me.
I am of the earth   and the earth is of me.

We are together   under the blue sky.
We are together   under the yellow
                                    sun.
We are together   under the gray
                                clouds.
We are together:
                sisters.

In both the families

In both the families
that
    both belong to me,
there is every shade
of
brown, and tan,
and paler
        honey,
creamy gold.

I face faces that I see
in
    both the families
that
    both belong to me,
and
they can face
my crooked
      grin.

Here is every shade of every color
                  skin.
    We fit in.

The way I see any hope for later

The way I see any hope for later,
we will have to get
                    over this color
                              thing,
and stop looking
              at how much brown
              or tan there is
                              in
              or on   this
                      woman
              or that   man.
And stop looking
              at who is a woman
                      and
                      who is a man.

Stop looking.
Start loving.

Remember:

Remember: long ago   before people moved
                and migrated, and mixed and
                                    matched
            their arms
side
    by
side
    in European caves;

    or captured slaves
were
sent in ships around this earth;

            long ago   there was one people:
                        one color,
                        one race.

Of the race

Some day   I will have babies with
high
foreheads   and curled
hair,
and darker places,
browner eyes.

The colors are flowing
from
what was before
me
to what will
be
after.

All the colors.

All the colors of the race

All the colors of the race. Human, of course.
　　　Beginning in Africa, in Asia, in the
　　　　　　　　　　　　　　　　Middle
　　　　　　　　　　　　　　　　East,

　　　and long before Plymouth
　　　　　　　　　　　Rock.

In ancient kingdoms the people are firing
　　　　　　　　　　clay heads for their gods;
　　　　　　　　　　　　　　　mixing
　　　　　　　colors
　　　　　　　for the headcloths
　　　　　　　of the mothers.

Mixing　　colors.
Mixing
　　　　　colors.

All the colors of the race. Human, of course.

Dedication:

For my children, Jaime and Leigh, and for their
brothers and sisters of every race
and every
wonderful combination of races.

Direction:

This book is a presentation of power and love.
Celebrate the meaning and music
of your lives.
Stand free and take control.

Library of Congress Cataloging in Publication Data.   Adoff, Arnold.   All the colors of the race.   Summary: A collection of poems written from the point of view of a child with a black mother and a white father.   1. Children's poetry, American.   2. Family—Juvenile poetry.   3. Race awareness—Juvenile poetry.   [1. American poetry.   2. Family— Poetry.   3. Race awareness—Poetry]   I. Steptoe, John, (date), ill.   II. Title. PS3551.D66A77   811'.54   81-11777
ISBN 0-688-00879-8   ISBN 0-688-00880-1 (lib. bdg.)   AACR2